ELMWOOD PARK PUBLIC LIBRARY
1 CONTI PARKWAY
ELMWOOD PARK, IL 60707
(708) 453-7645

1. A fine is charged for each day a book is kept
   beyond the due date. The Library Board may
   take legal action if books are not returned
   within three months

2. Books damaged beyond reasonable wear
   shall be paid for.

3. Each borrower is responsible for all books
   charged on this card and for all fines accruing
   on the same.

And they all lived happily ever after.

They lived happily ever after because...

the soggy knight fell in love with the clever Princess.

The knight fell in love with the princess because . . .

she poured a big bowl of lemonade on top of his head.

She poured a bowl of lemonade on top of his head because . . .

the knight's curly red beard was on fire.

His curly red beard was on fire because...

he had been tickling a great green dragon.

He had been tickling a great green dragon because . . .

the dragon would not stop crying.

The dragon would not stop crying because . . .

one hundred bunny rabbits had hopped into his cave and frightened him.

One hundred bunny rabbits had hopped into the dragon's cave because . . .

they were trying to escape an enormous tomato rolling down the hill.

An enormous tomato was rolling down the hill because...

it had been hit by a flying teacup.

It had been hit by a flying teacup because . . .

a hungry giant was throwing a temper tantrum.

The giant was throwing a tantrum because . . .

there were no lemons

left at the market.

And there were no lemons

left at the market because...

once upon a time a clever princess

decided to make a big bowl of lemonade.

To Laurie Skiba
—D.L.
To Denise for her famous
flat lemon cake
—R.E.

Library of Congress Cataloging-in-Publication Data

LaRochelle, David.
The end / by David LaRochelle ; illustrated by Richard Egielski. —1st ed.   p. cm.
Summary: When a princess makes some lemonade, she starts a chain of events involving a fire-breathing dragon, one hundred rabbits, a hungry giant, and a handsome knight.
ISBN-13: 978-0-439-64011-4   ISBN-10: 0-439-64011-3
[1. Fairy tales.] I. Egielski, Richard, ill. II. Title.
PZ8.L32837End 2006   [E]—dc22   2005024044

Book design by Elizabeth B. Parisi · Hand-lettering by Georgia Deaver · First edition, January 2007 · Printed in Singapore 46

THE

Story by David LaRochelle

🏮 Arthur A. Levine Books

END

Illustrations by Richard Egielski

An Imprint of Scholastic Inc.